Welcome to my Madness

Elida Y. García-DeHaan

ISBN: 9798841983118

DEDICATION

This book is dedicated to all who have supported my creativity and some of these poems/short stories of this book.

DISCLAIMER

Names and locations have been changed in some of these stories. These stories in this book have a darker theme/undertone.

ENERGY VAMPIRES EVERYWHERE

Energy vampires are everywhere.

Energy vampires are real.

They go about draining their victims of their energy and emotional well-being.

Energy vampires are everywhere.

Most energy vampires are those nearest and dearest to their prey.

They watch and wait for the time to strike.

Energy vampires do not care what their victims become once they've sucked the energy out of them.

They move onto the next victim as soon as they're done with their current prey.

Energy vampires are real.

They take and take every bit of energy they want.

Energy vampires everywhere, so beware.

HAUNTED BY HORROR MOVIES

I'm haunted by horror movies that are clearly not real.

Movies with blood, guts, gore, and serial killers.

Movies that are based on reality… where psychopaths hunt and stalk their prey.

Movies with the typical blonde female or ditzy women who get killed in the beginning of the movie.

Horror movies that portray endangered animals as vicious killers.

I'm haunted by horror movies with killer clowns who trick their prey into their grasp by enticing them with goodies.

These movies haunt me more than horror films based on true events such as paranormal events and demonic encounters. I've lived in that reality more times than I want to count.

I'm haunted by horror movies about teens getting murdered by a lake or at a party more than movies about ghosts and exorcisms.

I'm haunted by horror movies even as an adult.

FERTILITY STRUGGLES

"You May or may not be able to have children, and if you ever conceive a child, there will be complications".

How can a doctor tell a 14-year-old teenager that they may never have children?

I left his office traumatized and in shock. Shock that I will never have children.

"We need to schedule her for surgery," he told my mother. Surgery to see what was going on with my reproductive organs.

On February 1, 2002, we found out that my ovaries were enlarged and full of cyst. He started me on birth control to keep the cysts from growing. I remember seeing the images of my ovaries at the post-op appointment.

I was an almost 15-year-old virgin who had to take birth control.

As I got older, I thought, "Would any man love me knowing that children would not be possible?"

Five years later I found that man. A man who would choose me over the life of a child.

"I wouldn't be able to care for a love a child if you

died during labor," he admitted as he held me at bay while trying not to cry.

This was a man who understood my health conditions.

A month later I was pregnant by a man who was willing to choose my life over a child, but we were no longer together. The pregnancy was complicated from the beginning.

I was on and out of the hospital during my entire pregnancy. Mainly due to heavy bleeding and infections

All the while the man who said he would choose over a child did not respond to my emails right away. If and when he did, we argued.

By the time he came home from deployment it was almost time for this miracle to be born. He showed little interest in the unborn child. In fact, he did not want to accept the child as his.

The night before my baby was born still, she would stop moving whenever he would place his hand over her. She gave one last kick that night and she was gone the next day.

I lost a good amount of blood that day giving birth to her, but I was unconscious. I don't remember the doctor taking the baby before I could see her.

He got to see her, and it was unfair that I did not see her.

A month later another miscarriage by the same

asshole.

After that pregnancy, I gave up all hope of ever becoming a mother. He left me for another woman who already had a son that he raised as his own before she gave him a child. After 2008 I had over seven miscarriages before I decided to try to conceive again.

After the second round of fertility medication, I had a nervous breakdown. I thought what was the point of living if could never be a mother?

My husband and I tried two more cycles of medication with no success. I went back on birth control to prevent anymore miscarriages.

Eventually I wanted to try once more, but who knows if it will work this time. Hopefully hope is not   lost.

MASK MAKING

In March 2020 the world came to a halt thanks to Covid-19. We didn't know what the hell was going on, or how to fight this disease.

We were told, "Wear a mask! Stay at home! Wash your hands! Stay 6ft apart!" We were told be careful especially if you have health issues.

If we had to leave the house, it was just to the store, hospital, appointments, etc....

April 5, 2020, my world came crashing down. My mom had told me that my second mom (her friend from middle school) was in the hospital with Covid. I had no idea of her condition or how to reach her family. She raised me temporarily as a pre-teen. She taught me about life, how to cook, take care of myself, and how to speak up for myself. I was her Mija (daughter).

She died that day of complications with Covid and diabetes.

After her death I thought of ways to help fight this shit, so I began to make cloth Facemasks for family, friends, and to communities who needed masks.

I wanted to make sure everyone was protected from this disease.

Every mask that I make, I keep her in mind. Her stepdaughter is the one who taught me how to sew by hand. She is my mask making inspiration.

LOSING MY DAMN MEMORY

When people hear memory loss, they say, "It's old age". They're not entirely wrong, but there's a group of people with memory loss that is due to mental health issues or stress. There are also different levels of memory loss.

"Mild short term memory loss," is what read on my VA rating breakdown. I knew it was coming, but I didn't want to accept it.

Sure, the signs where there, but again I did not want to accept the fact that I was losing my damn memory.

My long-term memory is good, but anything after the last traumatic event is hard to remember.

It sucks that I can no longer multitask or have multiple conversations at once.

I hate having to write things down before I "forget." Heaven forbid I forget to write down a task or appointment because it happens, I end up scheduling multiple appointments on the same day.

I hate losing my damn memory. I find comfort in staying in past memories.

Memories of simpler times... a time when things

made sense.
Sure, the doctors can give me tools on how to slow the process down of memory loss, but it does not help me cope with losing my damn memory.

I STAND FROZEN

I stand frozen in the school supply section thinking of what notebooks, pens, folders, and binders you would want for school.
I stand frozen thinking what backpack you would want to carry your school supplies in.
I stand frozen thinking of gym shoes you would like to wear.
I stand frozen thinking of what high school would be like for you. Would you like it?
 Would you make lots of friends?
Would you like or dislike your classes?
Would you join a club?
Would you like your teachers?
I stand frozen thinking how life is unfair.
I stand frozen thinking of how you should be here to help me answer these questions.
I stand frozen missing you.
I stand frozen in time.
I   stand   frozen.

TAPS

Every night I hear a tune that is played at military and veteran funeral.

Every night I hear a tune for those who have made the ultimate sacrifice to this country.

Every night I hear this tune and think of all who came before me. I am grateful for their sacrifice and their service.

Every night I hear Taps, and it reminds me of how fragile life can be.

Every night I hear Taps before I sleep.

HAUNTED CAMILLE COURT

In 1979 a young girl, who had a complicated relationship with her mother, decided to play with the Ouija Board©™.
She had been cursed by her mother and friends of her mother. Cursed to fail and to do nothing with her life.
They left the door open to something evil.
This young girl ended up opening a portal between this work and the afterlife in order to numb her feelings towards her mother.
She was haunted by spirits, but no one knew what kind of spirits. Some say she was possessed by demons, and others say it was the father of evil.
Her parents took her to churches for cleansing and exorcisms.
The family eventually moved, but they could not rid the area of what came out of the portal that she opened. Those spirits still haunt Camille Court.
The grass never grows around that house.
There's an evil presence around that neighborhood.
It is a presence so thick that it can be felt while driving by that street.

People move in and out of that house afraid.
Afraid of what those spirits stay in that house.
Spirits that were never sent away... Spirits that will
remain   forever.

BACK TO THE DESERT TO FACE MY PAST

In 2006 my virtue aka my virginity was taken by a stranger. A stranger to me, but he was the friend of a friend.

I had no one to turn to for help, so I ran away from my happy place. A place where I found myself, and where I found my self-esteem.

I ran away from myself and hid for fifteen years.

"Let's move back to Arizona," blurted my mother after my husband asked me about housing prices in Arizona for shits and giggles.

Then it hit me... I need to face my past. I can no longer hid from things and people who had hurt me deeply.

One night around midnight I called the police department where the crime had taken place. "I need to report a crime," I said as the detective answered the phone. He gave me the usual round of questions, "Why didn't you not report the crime then?" "When did it happen?" "Where did it happen?" "Who were the people involved?"

I gave him as much information as possible and as

many details as I could remember. "I have everything I need. A detective will call you if they take the case since it has been almost fifteen years since this crime occurred.

"I understand officer". I hung up and then it was time to wait. While I waited, I put my house on the market and started to look for a new home. A home in the state that I love... Arizona.

Three months later I was back in the desert waiting for our new home to ours. A home that was far from where my virginity was taken.

A week later the nightmares began. Nightmares not related to the crime or perpetrator, but people who are connected to the perpetrator. In these dreams they were trying to hunt me down and kill me.

It dawned on me that in all my years of therapy not once did I talk about those involved in the rape. I rarely spoke about the rape itself in therapy.

During my time away from the desert friends would ask why I left, or when was I coming back to visit, but all of that changed once I was back in the desert.

Most have been told the real reason for my departure from Arizona, but they doubt me. They can't believe that someone they grew up with would endanger another person.

Now one calls or replies to my messages now that I

am back home.

Now I am back in the desert finding new friends and hoping to reconnect with people who would believe me. I am back in the desert to find myself once again... the girl who did not give a fuck.

CENTURIES' OLD LOVE

"We can run away together," the witch pleaded to her vampire lover, as the townspeople marched to their cottage in the woods.

"They will find us my love," he whispered back.

He held her tightly as the townspeople busted open the door. They stabbed him in the heart through his back and yanked her out of his arms.

She screamed in pain as they dragged her out of their home and tied her to the stake.

"Ella May Coors, you are convicted of being a witch. You will burn in hell for all eternity along with your vampire lover," said the clergyman before setting her on fire.

She continued to scream in pain... pain from losing the love her life.

Four hundred years later she was reborn as Elsa Marie Coors along with her vampire lover. She was a practicing witch who followed family traditions, and who working as a logistical clerk.

One day at the warehouse where she worked the communications manager came to the staff lounge to talk to Elsa, but he was nervous.

He sat down across from her before speaking, "Hey Elsa how's your day going?"

Surprised that he knew who she was she replied,

"I'm good and yourself Edwin?"

She blushed waiting for a response. "I am doing well. Thank you for asking," he paused trying to figure out how to ask her out on a date, "I was wondering if you would like to go out to dinner with me this evening?"

"Uh, a date?"

"Yes, a date with me?"

"Sure".

He was surprised that she would agree to go on a date with him. They had been drawn to each other for some time, but they didn't know to speak to each other.

"I can meet you here after work or I can meet you at the restaurant near the Port of Tacoma?"

"We can meet at the restaurant near the port". She wanted to say more, but her lunch was over and had to get back to her section of the warehouse. They went back to their parts of the warehouse, but he was on her mind as she separated items.

Later that evening she met Edwin outside the restaurant while he waited to be seated.

"You look unrecognizable," he blurted out wishing he could take that statement back.

Elsa replied bluntly, "Well duh, I'm not in my work clothes", as she twirled in her flowy pink dress.

"I am so sorry. I did not mean to say what I said".

"No worries. I know you meant no harm. Shall we

go inside?"

There was sincerity in his voice as he apologized repeatedly the whole way to their table. Elsa felt at home when she looked into his eyes.

Being the bold woman that she was she spoke first while they waited for their food. "So how did you end up here in Washington?"

"Is it that obvious that I am not from around here?"

"Yes, but I've heard people in the warehouse talk about others all day long".

"Oh, okay. Well, I was stationed at Fort Lewis a few years ago and decided to stay here once I got out of the army. You?"

Elsa was surprised to know that he knew that she wasn't from Washington either. "Same as you, but my family is from Massachusetts".

Just then a light in his head went off in his head, there was the connection between them, "Mine too, but sometime in the 1900s they left and moved south".

Elsa began to tell the story of her family as the food arrived at their table. Then she thought to herself, why was she telling her family history to a stranger?

"So, your ancestors were witches?"

"Well only one. She was in love with a vampire from Transylvania. Legend is that she wanted to run away with him, but he was stabbed in from behind as he held her in his arms".

At that moment, he felt a pain in his back, but he ignored it and continued to listen to her story. "What happened to her?"

"She was yanked from his arms, and they burned her at the stake".

She closed her eyes and tried to imagine what pain her ancestor had felt as her love died. Edwin interrupted her thoughts, "Are you okay?"

"Oh, yes. Sorry. Sometimes when I think about her story, I imagine the pain she felt. Then again, now but she would know what it felt like?"

He watched as she came back to reality. They continued their meal with some silence.

Edwin and Elsa not only shared a connection to their military career, but they both had a connection to Massachusetts.

After dinner they parted ways, "Thank you for dinner".

"You're welcome. I will see you at work".

He shook her hand and they exchanged goodnights. Once she was in her car, she felt relieved and took a deep breath. There was something about Edwin that gave her butterflies especially when she thought of him. Edwin felt the same way about Elsa, but either one of them did not know how to tell each other.

When he got home that night, he remembered an

old tale that his grandfather told him when he was little boy. "Many centuries ago, our family hid from the light and all humans because if people found out, they would be killed".

"Does that mean we come from vampires?"

"Yes, my boy, but they're long gone. There was only a handful of them. The last one was killed over four hundred years ago. He was stabbed in the back, but that is all I know".

It hit him like a mac truck, "her great ancestor's true love was related to his family!" Could it be possible that they were the reincarnated versions of their ancestors? He ran to the mirror to look at his birthmark... the mark look liked a stab wound, but how could he tell her the truth about their ancestors.

Back at Elsa's home she went through Ella May's books in order to feel closer to her. She always felt a connection to her especially because she was born a witch. She found love letters from Ella's vampire lover tucked in the back of her Book of Spells along with a photo that was taken of them. Elsa was caught off guard by how much the vampire resembled Edwin. He looks just like Edwin, she thought to herself. She needed to talk to him as soon as possible.

Edwin was getting into bed as his phone rang. "Elsa? Is everything alright?"

"Yes, sorry for calling late, but I need to see you".
"Sure. Would you like me to come over or do you want to come over to my place?"
"I think it is best for you to come over to my place".
She sounded concerned and it worried him, "Okay. I will be right over".
"I will text you my address and gate code".

30 minuets later there was a knock on her door. "Come in", she said as she guided him into the living room. He seen the photo of his ancestor on the coffee table.
"I take it, this is the reason you wanted me to come over?"
She nodded and didn't say a word as she sat next to Edwin. "Yes, and these are my great-great-great aunt's spell books, personal journals, and love letters from the man in the photo".
"Why do you have these? Are you a witch too?"
She took a deep breath, "These were passed down to me, and yes I am a witch, but I wanted to talk about this picture".
He cut her off, "I have a confession of my own".
She looked confused at him before he continued his confession.
"When I got home after our date, I remembered a story that my grandfather told me as a child. Our family came from vampires, or at least most of our

family members were vampires. This man in the photo was the remaining vampire".
They looked at each other trying to put the pieces the together.
"What does this mean?"
"I don't know Elsa, but maybe we can find out together".
"Does this mean you want to spend more time with me?"
"I would like to spend more time with you, but I'm wondering if we may be a reincarnated version of this couple".
"How is that possible?"
Edwin lifted his shirt and showed his birth mark on his chest. It was identical mark to where the stake was used on the lover of her great-great-great grandmother.
They sat and talked for hours about the story of his family as explained by his grandfather.
"You look like your ancestor," he blurted out while looking at the photo of her great-great-great aunt.
She shrugged at his comment. He was concerned, "did I say something wrong?"
"My relatives always say that about me".
He apologized, but she let him know that he didn't hurt her feelings.
"I should get going," he said looking at the clock realizing it was after midnight.

She stood up and walked him to the door, "Thank you for coming over".

After Edwin left she went to bed and was visited by her ancestor, Ella May Coors in her dream.

"Have you found your match my sweet girl?"

"Are you referring to Edwin?"

She nodded, "Yes, my girl. He is your match".

"But how? We have only been working in the same warehouse for six months, and we had our first date this evening".

Ella placed her arm around Elsa's shoulder, "You were destined to meet".

"What are you talking about?"

"Well the day that I died, I created a spell that would reunite the soul of myself and my vampire lover when the time was right. A time where witches and vampires could live freely".

Elsa thanked her ancestor, but told her aunt that it was still unsafe for vampires to live freely even though people watched vampires in movies and tv. She also let her that some religions still hated witches and seen them as evil or demonic.

"Yes, but this century is much different then mine. Please give this relationship a try. You were meant for each other my girl".

"Thank you".

"No, thank you my girl for taking care of my belongings and for continuing my path of magic".

Before Elsa could say more, her aunt was gone and her alarm went off.

Later on that day Edwin called his grandfather to tell him about Elsa and her family history.

"You have found her my boy!"

"What are you talking about grandfather?"

"Your true love. She is the reincarnated soul of the lover of our vampire ancestor. You have found the witch who bound your past souls together", he paused for jokingly saying, "When is the wedding?"

"What wedding? We went on our first date last night".

"Oh fine. When can I meet her?"

"Meet her?"

"I would like to welcome her to the family".

"It's too soon for that, but I will ask her if she would like to meet you old man," he joked. During the remainder of their conversation Elsa called. "I have to take this call grandfather".

"Hello Elsa, how are you doing today?"

"Still in shock about the connection between us, but more so about a dream I had after you left last night".

"Dream?"

"My great-great-great aunt came to visit me in my dream".

"What was it about?"

Elsa sighed, "I was told that you were my true match. I know that sounds weird especially since we just had our first date.".

"Not weird at all. My grandfather said the same thing before I answered your phone call".

"You told your grandfather about me? Why?"

"What else did he have to say?"

Edwin laughed as he answered her question, "When are we getting married?"

She chuckled back, "Marriage? How about we date a little more before we talk about marriage".

Her answer caught him off guard. "You want to marry me?"

"Someday, but not any time soon".

"Really?"

"Yes I do Edwin because we first met I felt like I've known you forever. I know that sounds cliché, but it's true".

"I feel the same way about you especially after we talked about the love of our past lives".

~

After several months of dating Edwin and Elsa were getting married at the location of the cottage of Ella May Coors in Salem, Massachusetts.

During their wedding ceremony, Elsa noticed two figures standing in the distance watching their dreams come true.

Their souls had finally been reunited at last.

Edwin and Elsa said their "I dos" in front of their loved ones and close friends.

 They were truly meant to be together forever

ABOUT THE AUTHOR

Elida is a multi-genre author who writes stories about her life in many forms, and she writes from the heart. Her books can be found online wherever books are sold.